First impression: 2002

Illustrations: Margaret Jones
Design: Olwen Fowler

Published with the financial support of the Welsh Arts Council

ISBN: 0 86243 605 2

Printed and published in Wales by
Y Lolfa Cyf., Talybont, Ceredigion SY24 5AP
e-mail ylolfa@ylolfa.com
web www.ylolfa.com
phone (01970) 832 304
fax 832 782
isdn 832 813

SAINT DAVID

by
Rhiannon Ifans

illustrations by
Margaret Jones

for
Gwyddno, Seiriol and Einion

Acknowledgements

The author wishes to thank Dr Gwyn Davies, Dr Menna Davies, Dafydd Ifans,
and Emeritus Professor R.M. Jones for their valued assistance during
the preparation of this book.

CONTENTS

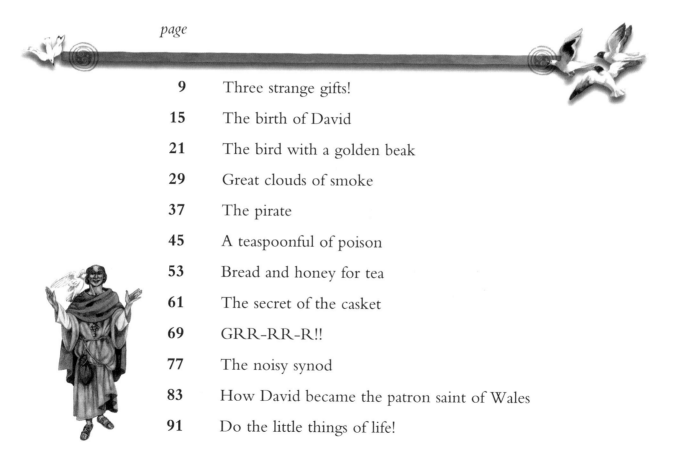

SAINT DAVID

This is a book about David, the most important of the Welsh saints.
No one knows very much about David, not for sure, but some reports
about him are certainly true. David lived in the sixth century. His mother's
name was Non, and his father's name may have been Sant. David came from
the south Ceredigion and north Pembrokeshire area, around St David's. He
was nicknamed 'David the water-drinker' because he loved to drink water.
Later, when he was grown up and had become a monk, he lived on very
simple food and drink. He may have died on 1 March 589.

Because he was such a fine man, many traditions grew up about him after
his death. They are all stories of praise. The people of long ago didn't care

whether the stories were true or not in a literal sense. But they were very careful that only stories of wonder and praise should be told about David, stories that honoured their fond memory of him.

All the old people remembered David as a strong and gentle man, and so they told tales that showed what an excellent man he was. Every person in the land remembered David as a mighty preacher, and so they told tales of what an eloquent man he was. They all remembered David as an adventurous leader, a much more daring and more important leader than even Owain Glyndŵr. They told marvellous tales about David in order to make that quite clear.

This book is full of amazing stories about David. It is a celebration of his life.

Three strange gifts!

Three strange gifts!

Sant, King of Ceredigion, had very cold feet. His flesh was a chilly blue. He untied his leather sandals and threw them to one side.

'Bedwyr!' he thundered. 'Come and wash my feet! That should warm them up!'

Sant was an ugly customer at the best of times. Safer to humour him. Bedwyr hurried over to the cauldron of hot water spluttering over the kitchen fire. He scampered up to Sant at full speed, hot water splashing over the sides of his golden bowl.

'It's like living on an iceberg here today, Your Majesty!' said Bedwyr slyly. Bedwyr was a lying dog. There was a cosy open fire on the floor of the old hall, its flames licking the glowing red logs.

'That's enough of your nonsense! Quickly! You scoundrel!' Sant growled sullenly.

Elen, the maid, appeared carrying a goblet of warm punch. But for the life of him Sant couldn't keep warm, no matter how he tried.

'This could be a sign, Your Majesty,' ventured Bedwyr. 'A vision! I've heard many people mention it. One minute they're chilled to the bone, fearing they'll catch pneumonia, and the next morning they're as fit as a fiddle – and they've seen grand visions!'

'Hmm. You may be right.' Sant was pacified.

Bedwyr dried his master's feet very thoroughly. He daren't upset him.
There was still a tinge of blue under his skin. In no time at all Sant had wrapped
himself up in a bearskin and was fast asleep.

When he awoke he was swathed in a strange light.

'Don't be afraid, Sant. I'm an angel and I have a message for you. Very soon
you will go hunting and find three gifts. You will kill a stag beside the river Teifi.
Your first gift. Then you will fish in the river and catch a salmon. Your second
gift. Before long you will find a hive of bees. Your third gift. Send a portion of
the stag, the salmon and the honeycomb to the monastery of Mawgan nearby.'

Sant gaped in astonishment. But the angel had more to say.

'These gifts are a sign that a son will be born to you in thirty years' time.
He will claim the land where you found the three gifts, and he will have three
personal virtues. The honey is a sign of his wisdom. The salmon is a sign that he
will live on bread and water instead of growing plump and fat on meat and wine.
The stag is a sign of his strength, and his ability to conquer bad spirits. Your son
will be the wonder of the land!'

'A son!' marvelled Sant. 'My own son!' He had no time to lounge around
in bed a moment longer. He pulled on his boots. He had work to do. Without
waiting for breakfast he snatched his bow and went riding on the banks of the
river Teifi.

Exactly as the angel had said, a strong stag wandered into Sant's path.

Sant shot him through the heart. The stag sank onto his forelegs, swayed like a bulrush in the breeze, and fell onto his side stone dead.

'Brilliant!' said Sant. His first gift.

Sant knew there were salmon in this part of the river. What a pity Bedwyr wasn't with him. There was no one quite like Bedwyr for catching salmon. Sant lay on his stomach, looking into the river. He had seen Bedwyr do this as he fished in the morning light. Sant's hands flew towards every salmon he could see. No luck. He tried several times to catch the fish in his hands, but they were far too clever for him. They flashed past him like arrows. He could swear they were making fun of him. Sad of heart, Sant cupped his hands and drank the river water to quench his thirst.

'Nothing will come of it!' said Sant wretchedly. He splashed his forehead with the cold water to revive himself. As he dried his eyes with a fistful of grass, he spotted a spear with a leather strap tied to it hidden away in the thicket.

'Perfect!' said Sant, tickling his chin.

He tied the leather strap around his waist and stood waiting for the salmon to jump. Soon a fat salmon leapt high over a jagged stone. Sant hurled the spear and it sank deep into the flesh of the dazzling fish. Then he pulled up the fish by the leather strap.

'Splendid!' said Sant. His second gift.

Sant rode his horse along the banks of the Teifi. Two out of three, and it wasn't even lunchtime! It would take him no time at all to find a swarm of bees. Didn't everyone who was anyone keep bees? There was a good chance that someone's bees had swarmed, forming a new colony on the banks of the river. The King of Ceredigion would claim them as his own.

It took half an hour, no more. Sant's horse marched straight into a swarm of the busiest bees anyone had ever seen. They stung the horse's knees. He was in so much agony his neighing echoed through the land. Sant didn't care. He was drunk with joy.

'Excellent!' said Sant. His third gift.

Before nightfall Sant had sent a large joint of stag and just as large a portion of salmon to Mawgan's monastery. With the meat he sent a honeycomb, the sweetest in Wales, safely stored in an earthenware jar. There at the monastery they would stay for thirty years. And then a son would be born.

'I wonder!' said Sant.

There was nothing for it but to wait and wait and see.

The birth of David

The birth of David

Sant lived the life of a king for thirty years. Each day he would think of the marvellous son that would be born to him. His child wouldn't be like the other babies of Ceredigion. No, indeed! His son wouldn't be a drippy little dunderhead. His son wouldn't squeal and bawl, his fists flailing. Sant knew exactly the sort of son he would have. A handsome little genius. What Sant did not know was who exactly his baby's mother would be.

One day, as Sant rode his horse in the land of Dyfed, he saw a very beautiful woman. Her name was Non. Sant was enchanted by her and fell head over heels in love. He dismounted and spoke to her with a silver tongue. He flirted with her on the warm grass. Non was appalled. But Sant was a strong and confident man. Against her wishes, Sant became the father of Non's child. From that moment forward Non ate nothing but bread and water.

Throughout her pregnancy Non attended church regularly. She loved listening to good men speaking about Jesus. She loved to hear about Jesus looking after his friends, and healing sick people. One morning Non went to church to pray for the birth of her baby. The church was very dark after the bright sunlight outside. But she could see the shadows of various friends listening to a tall, thin monk who stood at the front. He was obviously in trouble.

The monk was busy soothing his throat. He tried his level best to preach to the congregation, but he couldn't speak a word. Each time he tried, the words stuck in his throat. The congregation stared at him in disbelief. 'Giving up on his sermon half way through! How extraordinary!'

This monk was the well-known saint, Gildas. The tall monk hushed the crowd with a wave of his hand. 'I can speak and read as well as anyone, but once I start preaching I'm totally tongue-tied,' he said. 'No matter. I know what I'll do. You go outside into the sunshine and I'll try to preach to an empty church.'

There was much mumbling and dragging of feet but before long the floor of the church was empty, and the tall monk was ready to preach to the bugs in the straw. But to no avail. Each time he opened his mouth he was struck dumb.

'If there's anyone at all in this church, hiding in the shadows, come forward at once,' he ordered in a loud voice.

'It's only me,' said Non. 'I came in to pray for my baby.' She wanted so much to hear the stories about Jesus Christ and to come to love him, she had stayed behind to listen with the bugs. When the villagers went out into the sunshine she had hidden herself behind the partition which divided the church in two, the men on one side and the women on the other, in case she missed a word of the tall monk's sermon.

'Go outside, Non, my dear,' said the tall monk gently, 'and ask the villagers to come in. You see, I can't preach in your presence. Your unborn son is far greater than I will ever be. It's impossible for me to preach to him even though he hasn't yet been born.'

'But you're Gildas! One of the best men in the world!' Non protested.

'Your child will be far greater,' said Gildas. 'God bless you both, and may the Lord be with you!'

Non turned away from him and went out into the heat of the day. In a trice the villagers were standing in church once more, Gildas preaching to his congregation with the voice of a giant.

At exactly that moment King Cynyr, Non's father, had gone to visit a magician. The magician told him that a strange boy would be born in his realm before long. He would grow up to be a powerful and wise man, and he would never eat meat. Cynyr was furious. Non's baby! Non never ate meat either! Cynyr hated them both. He became so jealous of the baby, he couldn't rest until the baby was dead.

'What if he takes over my kingdom! I won't have it! This new baby won't live long! Over my dead body!'

Having learned from the magician where the new baby was to be born, Cynyr decided to keep watch over the site day and night. Cynyr knew exactly how he would kill the child. He would choke the baby with his two thumbs. It would all be over before the baby could even scream in fright.

As the time for the birth drew near, Non went out for a walk along that very road where Cynyr was keeping watch. As she went through a gap in the hedge

into a field, the sky darkened. A gusty wind blew up. The yellow flowers in the hedges reeled and their bells pealed brightly in the afternoon air.

Clutching at her shawl, Non bowed her head at an angle into the wind, which pulled at the fringes of her nursing shawl. Lightning flashed like glistening knives, and great claps of thunder terrified the hares in their dens. Rain crashed down from the sky in bucketfuls. No man or animal could stay out of doors in such a violent storm.

With the exception of Non. That first gust of wind passed her by. And then the place where she gave birth to her baby, and that spot only, was drenched in warm sunlight. The ground where she lay was soft and warm. As she gave birth to her baby, Non pressed her hand against a stone. She left the mark of her hand on the stone as though impressed on wax. A stray shaft of lightning split that stone in two. One piece leapt over her and stood proudly at her feet. In that place the Church of Saint Non was built, the stone being part of the altar.

Soon after, Non's little baby was baptised. The bishop named the child Dewi, or David.

David thrived a little more each day, there in the wild valley in the depths of Wales, where the yellow flowers sang in the hedges during daytime, and where the stars shone on the hilltops all night.

The bird with a golden beak

The bird with a golden beak

After a huge breakfast of eggs, rolls, honey, and fresh goat's milk, Ioan was ready to set off for school. His mother cleared away the wooden plates and snatched Ioan's cup from his hand almost before he had finished his drink.

'Will you get out of the house this instant,' said his mother. 'The last thing I want to see this fine morning is that monk coming down here complaining that you're late AGAIN!'

Ioan could count himself lucky that he was allowed anywhere near the school of Gweslan the monk. But Ioan had other views on the matter. If it were up to him he would be out clearing the fields of stones and weeds ready for his father to plough and seed. Even combing wool for his mother, with all the fleas and lice involved in that task, was better than school. His mother encouraged him out of the house with a smack of the dishcloth.

'I'm on my way!'

Ioan stumbled out through the door just as his mother was urging him to call for his friend David to keep him company. She wanted to make quite sure that Ioan would take the dirt track to the monk's school, and not go rushing out with a sickle to cut his way through the thicket, his mind full of plans to reclaim more wilderness for his father to cultivate.

'Come on, David! You lazy lump! Quickly!' called Ioan.

The two friends ran as fast as their scratched little legs could carry them, along the narrow path overgrown with brambles and wild roses, leading down to the yew trees. In that quiet glade was the monk's school. That is where Gweslan expected the two friends to learn the alphabet. That is where they were taught church rituals. And in the green light that battled its way through the dark branches of those old, old yew trees, the two boys learned the chants of the church.

'I'd rather learn how to chase birds. And how to kill snakes.'

'Gweslan wouldn't have a clue how to kill snakes.'

'Or how to scamper uphill. He couldn't outdistance a snail,' said Ioan with a giggle.

Gweslan was very old. He had grown so fat, he huffed and puffed when he had to bend down to pick up his quill. Gweslan chasing birds! What a joke! Tears washed down their faces.

'Cry-baby! Cry-baby! Come on, David. Race you to the classroom.' The two friends scurried down the path.

Ioan and David were the last to arrive. The monk's beady eyes watched the boys as they swept in through the school door. Gweslan's eyes were bruised through lack of sleep. The monk always slept on a bare floor. He must have got up last night, washed himself with freezing cold water, and prayed at the altar until morning picked its way through the darkness. That is what monks often did. Ioan and David would have to be very careful. No good would come of

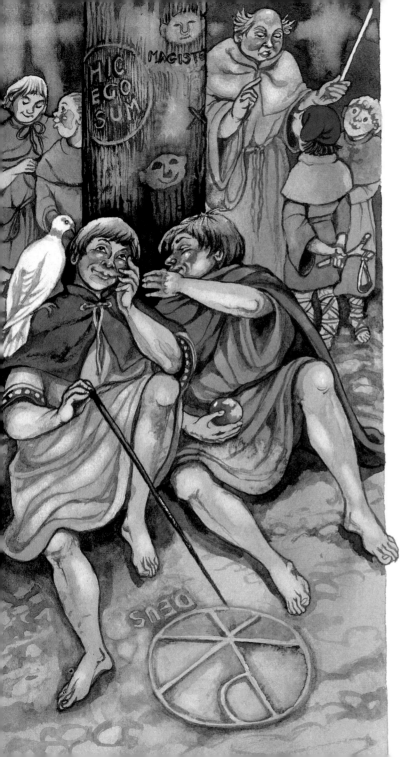

misbehaving today. The old monk's
patience had worn thin.

As if it could read their minds,
a beautiful bird flew in through
the open door. It flew around the
classroom three times. It was a very
strange bird. Not one of those black
and white magpies come to snatch
the monk's staff. Not a bullfinch
come to boast its feathers of fire.
Not one of the doves they could see
cooing in the dovecote outside the
monastery. But a strange, foreign bird.
It was a dove with a golden beak.

The bird settled on David's
shoulder. Gweslan took no notice
of it. In fact, it was as if he had been
expecting it to come. Gweslan had
cheered up no end and they all had
a happy day in spite of the bruises
under the old man's eyes.

The bird with the golden beak became a great friend of David's. Each time Gweslan taught the class a new psalm, the bird with the golden beak whispered in David's ear and helped him to learn it.

'God is our refuge and strength,' said Gweslan.

'God is our refuge and strength,' trilled the bird with the golden beak in David's ear.

'God is our refuge and strength,' said David, his voice as clear as a bell. David never faltered.

Autumn came early that year. Ioan and David helped Ioan's mother gather the apples in the orchard.

'What do you get hanging from apple trees?' asked David as he wiped away the apple juice that ran down his chin and onto his tunic.

'I don't know. What do you get hanging from apple trees?'

'Sore arms!'

Through their laughter they could see Gweslan making his way slowly towards them. He waved and the boys sobered up at once. But Gweslan didn't stop at Ioan's house.

'It's your mother he's visiting, not mine,' said Ioan. 'I wonder what he wants. Let's go and listen at the door.'

And that is how the two boys heard the news that David was to be moved to another school. Gweslan's plan was that David should be sent from Henfynyw school to a school at The Old Bush. The abbot there was Paulinus, and from now on he would be David's teacher.

David loved his new school. He loved the worn out, concave steps which led up to the abbey church. He loved looking out through the pointed windows at the red kite hovering and circling in the breeze. But more than that he loved his lessons. He loved the story of Easter most of all.

Early on Easter Sunday, Paulinus, all the monks of the abbey, and all the abbey pupils, worshipped together. There was a brilliant white cloth on the altar, and a golden cross at its centre. Paulinus chanted verses from the Bible. David knew them all by heart.

Paulinus was busy with his preparations to commemorate the life of Jesus. Jesus had been punished by God, and had died, to spare ordinary people from having to suffer for their own misdeeds. Paulinus blessed the bread and wine. Easter Sunday was a very important day. Each person took a piece of bread, and took a sip of wine, to show they believed that Jesus, after he had truly died, had risen from the grave – ALIVE! That was the best bit of the whole year for David.

But then, every day at Paulinus's school was good.

One night Paulinus suffered terrible pains in both his eyes. By morning his sore eyes had become inflamed. Paulinus winced as the pale light of morning came in through the window of his cell.

Paulinus called together all his pupils to see whether anyone could heal him.

He was by now blind. Each one in turn prayed for strength to heal his master's sight. One by one they returned to their cells. No one could cure Paulinus. The only pupil who had not attempted to do so was David. He was called forward.

'No!' said David. 'I couldn't. I've been here for ten years, reading with Paulinus, but in all that time I've never looked at my master's face. I would be far too shy to touch his eyes. Ask someone else.'

'If you're too shy to look at me, then touch my eyes without looking,' said Paulinus. 'If you do that, I'm sure I'll be able to see perfectly well.'

David prayed for God's strength. He touched Paulinus's blind eyes. And in that instant the aching eyes were healed and Paulinus's sight was restored.

Great clouds of smoke

Great clouds of smoke

David made his way very slowly up the steep slope to the monastery. He could see it clearly from where he stood at the bottom of the cliff. Stormy winds swept in from the sea, twisting and squirming inside David's habit, shaking his very bones. David rested on his walking-staff. He was tired. He was on his return journey from Brittany and after arriving in Wales he had walked every step of the way. One more effort and he would be home safe and sound in his old monastery at The Old Bush.

But for David things would never be the same again. In the year 547 a terrible plague, the Yellow Plague, had broken out in Wales. David had fled for his life. He crossed the sea to Brittany with his mother, Non. But Non never returned to Wales. She died near Landerneau in Brittany. No, things would never, ever be the same again.

David could see someone looking down at him from the monastery door. A kind face, smiling broadly. Could it be … ? It was! Gweslan, his old teacher in Henfynyw monastery. He was still alive and well in spite of the Yellow Plague!

'Come on, lazybones!' called an encouraging voice. With a hop, skip and a jump David crossed the threshold of the monastery, clutching the outstretched hands of his old friend.

David enjoyed his welcome home. Masses of warm crunchy bread and a jug of clear water from the well. Travellers were always served fish and tender meat at all the monasteries where they called, and offered butter and vegetables. The table groaned under its heavy load. But David would only eat bread and water, even after his exhausting journey.

'You haven't changed a bit, David!' said Gweslan proudly.

'Strange you should mention it,' answered David, 'since I'm on the brink of a mighty change in my life.'

'Oh?'

David wandered over to the window. 'Look out towards Porth-clais, Gweslan,' he said.

'There isn't a better view throughout the land,' said Gweslan.

'But don't you see how dangerous a site this is? Pirate ships could easily come into the harbour any day of the week – or at dead of night. The pirates would creep up the slope, and kill us all in less than fifteen minutes. There's hardly a more dangerous spot in the whole of Wales.'

'What do you intend to do about that?' asked a bewildered Gweslan.

'Move,' said David. 'Move further inland and settle in a spot hidden from the sea, out of sight of pirates, and less exposed to storms. What about it?'

'I don't know what to think,' said Gweslan. He thought hard, his face crumpled like a handkerchief.

'Good idea?' asked David.

Finally Gweslan agreed. 'I rather think it is,' he said, and thumped the table.

David, his old teacher Gweslan, Aidan, Teilo and Ismael his best friends, and all the other monks, packed their bags and carried them on their backs to a safe place. This was Glyn Rhosin. This was where their home was to be. Meanwhile, as night drew in, they could do nothing more than eat their bread and drink their water, before falling fast asleep.

A little before dawn on the following day, David woke up. It was a bitterly cold morning, and his limbs were stiff and aching. But he had much to look forward to. His hands wouldn't be numb for much longer. His particular job for the day was to light a fire. This wasn't just any old fire that he had to prepare. It was to be a very special, ceremonial fire. This fire would signify that he, David, was going to settle in the vicinity. Wherever the smoke from his fire travelled, he would claim that land for himself. That was the usual way of claiming ownership. On this land he would build a simple monastery for himself and his disciples.

He woke up his friends and they hurried to collect sticks for firewood. Their breath trailed white after them as the pale morning light trickled into the world. Soon, flames were leaping from the mound of wood. David's friends used damp wood once the fire had got going. The smoke almost choked them all. Thick clouds of swirling smoke rose up from their fire, covering the whole area by lunchtime, covering the whole of Wales by late afternoon, and then covering parts of Ireland by nightfall.

Bwya could hardly not notice it. Bwya was an Irish chieftain who lived opposite the spot where David had lit his fire. He was also a druid and he understood David's message. Great clouds of smoke had encircled Bwya's land and home. He was not a happy man. In fact, he was in a very bad temper. He sat on a high rock watching the smoke encircle the land. All day long he sat there, not able to touch a scrap of food.

Satrapa, his wife, was a very hard lady. At first she couldn't find Bwya to complain to him about all the smoke that was ruining the day for her. Eventually she found him sitting all alone on the rock.

'Why are you sitting here?' she asked.

'Just watching the smoke,' he said gloomily. 'It's coming from Glyn Rhosin. There must be someone there. He's claiming the land. Every piece of land and every blade of grass that the smoke encircles will be his.'

'But you can't allow that to happen,' said Satrapa. If she was angry about the smoke before, she was even angrier now. She turned on Bwya. 'You must fight this man.' She grabbed his shoulder. 'Stir yourself! Call your men! Kill this person! How dare he light this fire on your land without your permission!'

Bwya had no choice but to listen to Satrapa's tirade for the rest of the day. He did as she ordered, calling his soldiers and commanding them to prepare for battle. By the next day the soldiers' armour gleamed and their horses neighed

and reared their heads as the excitement in the camp mounted. They were all eager to kill David and his disciples.

They rode as far as David's camp. Just as they were ready to attack, a strange illness gripped them. The soldiers' arms went as limp as rags. Their whole bodies sagged with weakness. They shivered and shook and it was as much as they could do to stay in their saddles. They were so weak, they could do nothing to hurt David or his disciples. All the soldiers could do was mock David and shout abuse at his friends. Eventually, these soldiers had to return to their camp, a very sorry sight indeed.

On their return journey, whom should they see coming to meet them but Satrapa. She was in a mad panic. Long before she got near them she shouted wildly at Bwya.

'Bwya! Bwya! Hurry home! A terrible thing has happened!'

'Satrapa! What's the matter?' asked Bwya.

'The shepherds tell me that all the animals are dead, every last one of them. The cows, oxen, sheep, stallions and mares, they're all lying dead in the fields, with their eyes wide open! Bwya! What will become of us?'

Bwya was shocked and afraid. His soldiers had been stricken with fever and couldn't lift a finger, and now his entire stock had been struck down in one blow.

'It must have something to do with that trespasser in the valley,' said Bwya.

'Bwya! What shall we do?'

'There's nothing we can do, is there? He must have supernatural powers to be able to perform such terrible things. He must be a saint,' said Bwya.

'But if he's a saint it's useless to go against him.'

'Exactly,' said Bwya. 'I must give him Glyn Rhosin before anything worse happens to me.'

So Satrapa and Bwya, much against their wishes, trudged along to David's camp. They apologised for bringing an army against David and promised that the land around Glyn Rhosin should be his. David was free to build a monastery there, and to live in peace and quiet with his disciples for the rest of his days. His successors also had permission to settle there for as long as they wished.

Bwya and Satrapa were disappointed about their loss, but they were secretly glad to have got off the hook so lightly. But that didn't stop them from mumbling and grumbling, and moaning and groaning all the way home.

When they got within earshot of the palace, they couldn't believe their ears. There was a terrible din coming from the surrounding fields. Their sheep and cattle, oxen and horses, had all come back to life again. They were neighing and moo-ing, baa-ing and lowing, as only hungry stock can do. And little wonder! They had missed a day's feed!

The pirate

The pirate

Satrapa was in bed resting on one elbow. Bwya was fast asleep beside her, having tossed and turned most of the night. Satrapa nudged his shoulder. Very slowly Bwya lifted one lazy eyebrow.

'Yes?' said Bwya cautiously. He knew Satrapa was annoyed. He could tell by the way that she sucked her teeth. He knew without opening his eyes that she had the look of thunder.

'I was upset yesterday,' said Satrapa. 'That's why that half-witted saint had his own way. But today … '

'What about today?' asked Bwya, his eyes by now like dinner-plates.

'Today is another day!'

Bwya waited to hear more. Satrapa said nothing. She kicked her legs out of bed and called her maids. Bwya sighed. Once he turned his back there would be no knowing what they were up to. Had he better stay at home to keep an eye on them? 'It wouldn't make a blind bit of difference to that wife of mine,' sighed Bwya once more. 'Not with all that spiteful hissing under her breath that's been going on lately.'

Satrapa had been planning all night. She had decided on tactics. No one would stand in her way.

'Go down to the river where that saint and his childish puppets are camping,'

Satrapa ordered her maids. 'We're going to shame them. Take your clothes off and bathe in the river. Those monks won't know where to look! You'll see! They'll run for their lives!'

The maids went down towards the river. The monks watched them making their way across the valley. When they came to within hearing distance, the women shouted rude remarks. The monks were embarrassed and irritated. When the women splashed about in the river, naked as the day they were born, the monks looked away. They called David.

'We can't stay here with these foolish women. We'll have to abandon this site and find another spot for our new monastery.'

The women smiled and winked as they watched the unhappy monks. Satrapa's plan was working!

But there was disappointment in store for them. David was a sensible man. He had not been unnerved by the women's flirting. He spoke quietly to his friends and they soon settled down. 'We shouldn't be overcome by evil, but overcome evil with good,' said David. 'It would be far better for the women to find another home. It's they who should leave, not us.' In three sentences David had persuaded his friends to stay.

Throughout that night the monks fasted. That is what monks did when they needed God's help to solve problems or to carry out good work – stop eating. David believed that was an excellent way of winning God's kindness, so they fasted all night, and prayed for help.

Over at the old fortress, Bwya spent another restless night. He knew his wife was up to something, but had no idea what her plans could be.

The following morning, when Bwya's back was turned, Satrapa went in search of her stepdaughter, Dunawd.

'Come and gather nuts with me,' said Satrapa.

'Of course,' said Dunawd. They took the path down into the valley. It was a warm afternoon. The two women dawdled in the hazel grove on the banks of the river Alun. They gathered a basketful of the best nuts and Satrapa sat on a smooth stone and paddled her feet in the river.

'Come and sit here,' she said. 'The sun is very hot.' Dunawd lay down on the grass and rested her head in Satrapa's lap. Without a word of warning Satrapa took out a knife from the pocket of her long gown. Its blade was like a flash of steel. Satrapa cut off Dunawd's hair and threw the strands into the river. Dunawd was Bwya's daughter. But to the druids, cutting off someone's hair was tantamount to adopting them. Dunawd was now Satrapa's daughter, and as a result, Satrapa could do as she wished with her.

Satrapa had promised her own gods, the Siddi, that she would kill Dunawd as a sacrifice. With the flashing knife Satrapa cut the girl's throat. The instant her blood hit the ground a well appeared on the spot, the Well of Dunawd, its waters flowing as clear as crystal.

A well! Satrapa was very frightened. She had not expected this. It was obvious that something strange was going on. A fountain springing up almost before Dunawd had died! Satrapa fled the country and no one ever saw her again.

Bwya climbed into bed that night a very disappointed man. His daughter and wife had disappeared. And there was a new fountain, so his soldiers said, down in the hazel grove on the banks of the river. The world had gone mad.

But that was not all. The sea birds noticed a boat coming quietly in towards the land. At the oars was a dangerous Irishman, hair down to his shoulders and dying for a fight. His name was Lisgi. He rowed the boat into a small dark bay. From that day forward the bay was called Porthlisgi.

Lisgi was a pirate and he was out for trouble. His men tied the boat securely to a piece of driftwood on the beach. They climbed the path up the steep slope, past the empty monastery, and on towards the secluded valley. There was a light in the old fortress. Lisgi and his men crept forward like black cats through the darkness. What a piece of luck! No watchmen on the fortress gates. They burst into the hall. The men scattered into the four corners of the palace. What a night! Treasure by the armful! Wow!

Lisgi stole upstairs. He came to the tower where Bwya was sleeping. Bwya stirred. Before he was properly awake Lisgi had cut off his head. Having stolen everything of value from the fortress, Lisgi set the walls of the wooden huts alight. The whole fortress burned right down to the ground.

Lisgi and his men
were half way back to
Ireland before anyone
knew they had called.

A teaspoonful of poison

A teaspoonful of poison

David leaned on his spade and looked out over the valley. Sweat trickled from his forehead and down his cheeks. The weary monk wiped his face with his habit. Digging ditches was heavy work with only a pick and shovel to hand. But David loved it. How many times had he encouraged the monks to work with their hands? 'He who does not work, let him not eat.' That was his sermon in church last night. If a monk expected to eat he would have to do some very hard work to earn his food. Plough the fields, cut the hay, grind the corn, feed the cattle, slaughter the pigs … everything! And that is why no one in the monastery ate a crumb before three o'clock in the afternoon.

There was more than enough work for them all. This newfangled idea of bringing in oxen to plough monastery land was pure nonsense. Strong monks could do the work just as well. David could do it himself! He gazed out over the valley at two young monks ploughing. Behind them opened long, straight furrows. They would have to wait until late afternoon before sowing the crops. By then the moon would be up and the rhythm of the moon would help the seeds to take root.

David knew everything about nature. He knew when to cut the timber on the slopes and how to work the wood, although most of the trees were little more than stumps, tough and bowed. He knew how to cut stones into squares

and how to build a strong wall that wouldn't fall down until the end of time. It was David and his friends who had built the stone monastery where they lived. People came from far and near to visit them there. Some travelled over mountains and dangerous swamps. Others travelled across the sea, at the mercy of currents and crosswinds and the vicious storms that battered the seacoast. Over the years they had entertained many oddballs. But the oddest of them all had been Sguthyn. And this is how it happened.

A long way away in Ireland, in the monastery of Wexford in the south, David's friend, Aidan, was in church praying. It was the night before Easter and he was preparing for the very important Easter Day services.

He was suddenly struck by the idea that all was not well with David over in Glyn Rhosin. Treachery! Exactly that. David was in great danger. There were no two ways about it. But who would be such a savage as to harm David?

Aidan rose from the altar a shaken man. David would have to be warned. Immediately. There wasn't a moment to lose. Aidan looked down towards the beach. No sign of a boat. What could he do? Whom could he send to warn David?

'There's nothing for it but to send one of the monks down to watch the beach,' said Aidan to himself. 'A fisherman might return to the harbour before long. I'm sure he would be willing to take one of our monks over to Wales.'

He called Sguthyn. 'Go down to the sea to wait for a fisherman. I want you to visit David at Glyn Rhosin as soon as possible. Someone is trying to kill him.

It's only you who can warn him. Only you can save his life. Try your best, and don't fail him.'

Sguthyn hurried down to the seashore. There wasn't a boat in sight. Sguthyn soon realised that the wind was in the wrong direction. Even if a fleet had landed and he had his choice of a dozen ships, he would never reach Wales by morning.

He would have to swim. Sguthyn tied his habit around his waist and stepped out into the sea. The waves lapped against his knees. He stepped further out. His toe touched a sea monster. Perfect! One of the ocean's biggest creatures! Sguthyn jumped on its back. He was carried safely across the sea to Wales in less time than Aidan would take to eat his supper. The monster hauled himself up to the beach at Porth-clais.

The following morning Sguthyn climbed up the cliff, walked past the old monastery, and travelled on into the tranquil valley where the monks were celebrating Easter. As David was leaving church after communion he saw Sguthyn coming to meet him. This would be a very happy Easter. One of Aidan's monks had come to visit. He hugged Sguthyn and welcomed him kindly.

When David understood why Sguthyn had come to visit him he became very quiet. He thanked God for giving him warning of what was about to happen. Immediately following the Easter services a sumptuous meal was to be held at the monastery. Someone intended to poison David at that very feast.

Come to think of it, more than one of the monks had recently accused David of being too strict. They complained they had to do the work of animals. They sulked because they had to pray on their knees on cold stone, sometimes for three hours, until their legs were numb and the blood couldn't get to their feet. They cried blue murder because they had to obey David's commands almost before he had finished giving them. If the monks were just about to read the tip of the first letter of a word, they had to get up quickly and leave what they were doing in order to obey David promptly. And for all their efforts they were rewarded with bread and lettuce leaves. More than one monk was creaking under the strain.

Three, in fact. The steward, the cook and the deacon had had enough. They wanted revenge. It was all the steward's idea. He was head of the monastery kitchen and it was his responsibility to work out what the monks would eat. The steward and the cook were great friends, and they plotted to poison David's bread. A teaspoonful of poison. That was all it would take. Every day David sat at the table in exactly the same place, in exactly the same chair. It would be easy to put poisoned bread on his plate.

But there was one greedy monk at the monastery. He was as fat as a pig. If there was ever one piece of bread left over on the wooden plate, you can be sure he would snatch the last piece from under the monks' noses and gobble at it hungrily with bulging cheeks. What if David wasted a chunk of his poisoned bread, and the greedy monk guzzled it? No, the deacon had better serve the bread to each monk separately. He could offer David the poisoned bread, and offer clean bread to everyone else. And so it was agreed.

When they were all seated at the table and grace had been said, the deacon stepped forward to serve David. He had the poisoned bread in his hands.

Sguthyn also stepped forward. 'I'm serving David at the Easter feast,' he said. 'You sit down and enjoy the fun.'

David took the poisoned bread and blessed it. He divided it in three. He gave one piece to a dog sniffing at the door. The dog died instantly. All its hairs fell on the floor, its skin fell on the grass, and its guts fell on the doorstep.

David fed the second piece of bread to a crow nesting in a rowan tree. The instant the crow ate the bread, it fell off the branch and dropped to the floor, dead for all to see.

There was one piece left. David blessed and ate it. The monks looked at him in fear. You could hear a pin drop. They all kept their eyes fixed on him for about three hours, expecting him to die at any moment.

But nothing happened. Nothing at all. David had an early night. The excitement of it all was almost too much for him.

B read and honey for tea

Bread and honey for tea

Things improved no end in the kitchen of Glyn Rhosin after the cook packed his bags and left. A new monk, an Irishman, took his place. His name was Myddyfnog, but everyone called him M.

No one could beat M's blackberry pudding. Every autumn the hedges of Glyn Rhosin were heavy with blackberries, some fat and ripe, others small and hard. M always sent someone out to pick fresh ones each morning. Sometimes M would catch them coming back with their hands and faces stained purple, but he never breathed a word.

Other times M would catch a fat bird roosting in one of the low trees on the hillside. He would have it plucked and roasted before mid-afternoon. On days like this the monks would light a fire and keep it burning for hours. M roasted each bird until its legs dropped off and until the smell of sage penetrated every corner of his large kitchen. No wonder the monks liked Mondays and Thursdays best of all. There was hope of meat and a cosy fire on those days, since they weren't such popular days for fasting. The trouble was you could be punished for eating in the kitchen when it wasn't an official mealtime – and M's cooking really was fit for a king. It was very difficult being a good monk all the time.

M loved bee-keeping best of all. He kept a hive of bees in the monastery garden. He cultivated flowers for the bees to suck their nectar. M loved listening

to the hum of bees as he picked
rosemary in the garden ready for tea.
There was no one quite like M for
collecting the honey from the hive
and pouring it into earthenware jars.
He used the honey to feed the monks
when fruit was scarce, and when all
the birds had long deserted the valley.

M could make a wonderful honey
drink. It was called mead. Preparing
mead was very difficult. M would strain
the mixture well in case anyone should
complain he had a thick head the next
morning. That was the trouble with
mead. One drop too much and they
would all be seeing double.

At the end of each summer
M would gather wax from the
beehives to make candles. M loved
thick candles. Altar candles. Quite
often during communion, or when

he ought to be reading psalms, M loved watching the flames dance. He loved watching the tongue of fire lunge when an unexpected draught shot from under the door. The very next minute the flame would spout its warm, golden rays on the altar cross.

One day, in addition to all his other work, M decided to spend some time working outside with his friends. They were hard at work creating a new cart-way leading up to the monastery door. The new road would be far more suitable than the old one, especially as so many visitors trundled their carts up to the monastery carrying sacks of food, high days and holidays.

M and his friends dug a solid foundation for their cart-way. Tegfael, one of the younger monks, rested on his shovel for a while, ready to boast his handiwork.

'Come on, Tegfael! We've no time to laze about! The work won't finish itself!' cajoled M.

'Me! Lazing around! You're no angel yourself!'

'Steady, Tegfael!' said M.

'Don't you have enough on your plate what with the kitchen and the bees and all that praying, without coming out here to tell us how to build a road?' Tegfael was angry. He was a dwarf of a man but had the strength of an ox. He was so angry he lifted up his shovel ready to knock M flat. David was watching from the monastery window. Before things got too serious he made a sign with his hand. Instantly, Tegfael's hand shrank to half its size.

Tegfael almost a murderer! That was a hard lesson for them to learn. M was very sorry he had gone out to work on the road that day. From then on he kept his feet firmly inside the monastery door, only stirring out for a breath of fresh air in the garden. Before long M felt a great longing for the open countryside of Ireland. He spoke to David one day about his homesickness.

'Sooner or later there comes a time when we should all return to our homeland,' said David kindly. 'Your time has come. Go in peace!'

M put some food and drink in his satchel and the monks accompanied him down to the end of the new cart-way. M then went on alone to the boat that would take him back to Ireland. As he got to Porth-clais beach he heard a hum behind him. Bees! The bees had swarmed and had come down to the beach to see him off. M climbed into the boat. The bees flew in after him.

How puzzling! M had no idea what to do. He couldn't take the bees on the boat to Ireland or David would be without mead and honey. He would have to persuade the bees to return to the monastery garden. M walked all the way back to the monastery. The bees followed his every step. Having settled them back into the beehive, M slipped down to the beach once more, but they still pestered him. The bees had swarmed a second time. For the second time M took them back to the monastery garden. Each time M ventured further than the end of the new cart-way, the bees followed him.

M went to David for advice.

'Don't look so guilty,' said David, his eyes twinkling. 'Take the bees with you! The garden is full of flowers. They are certain to attract another swarm.'

David turned to the bees and blessed them. This time M went all the way down to the beach, jumped into the boat, and sailed across the sea to Ireland, his faithful bees in tow. And that was the first time that bees had ever been seen in the Emerald Isle, and the first time that Irish monks had bread and honey for tea.

The secret of the casket

The secret of the casket

Night was closing in. Dusk tucked itself in like a warm, grey blanket, wrapping itself around them. David lay on his back looking at the stars. How awesome! Beside him Teilo and Padarn snored lightly. The lilt of the sea still had them in its grip and had lulled them to sleep.

At last! thought David.

He had dreamt of this day for a long, long while. He had longed for this day year after year. At last David had crossed the English Channel and was spending the night in the land of Gaul. He was on his way to Jerusalem, to Palestine, the land of Jesus. At last he would see the Church of the Holy Sepulchre where Jesus was buried and raised up. He would prove his love for Jesus by walking every step of the way to visit his tomb.

David would then be allowed to wear a badge shaped like a palm-leaf. A pilgrim who had journeyed to Spain, to visit the tomb of Saint James in Santiago de Compostela, could pin a badge shaped like a shell to his hat, but only a pilgrim who had been to Jerusalem and had stood by Jesus' tomb could wear a palm-leaf. David couldn't wait.

But the three friends had a long and dangerous journey ahead of them. David needed his sleep. He closed his eyes and dreamt once more of the Holy City.

The next morning, as David, Teilo and Padarn rose from their prayers, they could hear some very harsh voices coming towards them. Another company of pilgrims! Where would they be going?

'Are you on your way to Jerusalem, my friends?' asked David.

'Some to Jerusalem, and some to Rome to visit the tomb of Saint Peter and the tomb of Saint Paul,' called a voice. 'And while we're at Jerusalem we hope to see the table where the Last Supper was eaten, and the veil which Jesus wore in the tomb. We could travel together part of the way if you like.'

'Excellent,' agreed David. 'Where do you people come from?' He had noticed some very odd goings-on at the back of the crowd. He really did wonder who they could be.

'Oh, we're Gauls. I'm Bernard. One of Pierre's men. Pierre the Black Prince.'

Bernard trundled a cart before him, with a beautifully carved casket sitting snugly inside. David couldn't stop gazing at the glamorous box. He stared at it harder still. There were pictures all around it. One very superb picture. It was of a soldier holding an axe. He was slipping its blade through the throat of a tall man who stood next to him. The head was about to topple over and fall flat on the floor.

'What's inside the box?' asked David weakly. He could hardly bear to hear the answer. Could this man be wheeling a skull to Jerusalem?

'AA-AA-GH!' There was a roar at the back of the crowd.

'What was that?' asked David. 'Is anyone in trouble? In pain?'

'Oh, it's only Pierre,'
said Bernard casually.

'What's the matter with him? Tell me!' David insisted.

'Go and see for yourself if you're such a busybody,' said Bernard.
'I'm sick of telling people.'

David moved towards the back of the crowd. Pierre the Black Prince
was fighting his way forward to Jerusalem and three monks were beating
him with branches.

'Have mercy, O Lord! Forgive this poor man, Pierre the Black Prince,'
he shouted half-heartedly in a broken voice.

'Forgive what, Pierre? What have you done to deserve this?'

The monks put down their branches. Pierre slumped onto the grass and licked his wounds.

'I'm travelling to Jerusalem to have my sins forgiven.' Pierre coughed blood.

'Take your time, Pierre,' said David, leaning down beside him to support his head. Pierre recovered a little and went on with his story.

'I've done some terrible things,' he said. 'I killed my son to stop him taking over my kingdom. Then I killed my wife. Wrenched her head off her shoulders.' Pierre fought for breath. 'She threatened to stab me through the heart with a dagger because I had killed our eldest son. I don't blame her. Time passed and now I'm old and weary. When I fell ill I turned to the monks for help. They say I must walk to Jerusalem to do penance, and tell my story to all that ask. They say I'll find forgiveness if only I can make it to Jerusalem, and my wounds will be healed in one of the holy wells of the city.'

'God is merciful and gentle. Ask God to forgive you at home. There's no need for you to go all the way to Jerusalem. You're an old man,' said David.

'Perhaps so, but I'd feel better if I made the effort. Thank you for your kindness, all the same.'

'Bless you,' said David sadly.

Why were these people so superstitious? With a quick step David made his way to the front of the crowd.

'Bernard!'

'Oh, it's you. I see you've finished snooping around at the back of the crowd. Did you get to know everything you wish to know?'

'Too much by far. People are so peculiar.'

'And now you've come to nose around in my cart, have you?'

'I may see more wonders in there than I've ever seen in my life.'

'Fine, mister-know-all.' Bernard put down his cart. He squared his shoulders and folded his arms. 'What have I got in this casket? You won't be happy until you know exactly what's in here.' Bernard brought his face up to David's. They were nose to nose. 'Guess!'

'A skull,' said David simply.

'Spot on!' said Bernard. 'But how did you know?'

David ignored his question. 'Whose skull?' he asked like a shot.

'Pierre's wife's,' said Bernard. 'Pierre believes that if she,' and he nodded at the remains of Pierre's wife, 'comes with us, he'll earn himself a worthier pardon. He intends to hang on to the skull just like the monks hang on to their relics, you know how they keep a piece of an important person's dead body to bring good luck.'

'Only fools believe that,' said David in dismay.

'Don't look at me,' said Bernard. 'This has nothing to do with me. I'm only here to push this cart.' He winked at David. 'And to enjoy the scenery.'

'What a peculiar man! Very peculiar indeed!' muttered David to himself. He looked around for Teilo and Padarn. He could see them at prayer. There was so much to pray for. David felt very small and insignificant.

GRR–RR–R!!

GRR-RR-R!!

Teilo licked his wrists eagerly. Mm-m-m. Lovely. Juice ran in torrents all over his hands and wrists. What was this fruit called again? A melon! That was it! There was nothing like it in Wales. Nothing at all. It was worth the journey to Palestine if only to taste a melon. Olive green skin. Reddish brown pips. Bright red flesh. And oceans of juice. Bliss!

Truth to tell, Teilo would have wolfed down whatever was put on his plate. All day every day he had that hungry look about him. And thirsty? His tongue was like a dried kipper. What with the scorching sun, and the dusty track going on and on into the distance, Teilo was dog-tired. He was tired in every one of his bones. Had the monks not established hostels within a day's journey of one another, Teilo would never have reached Jerusalem.

They were good hostels, very welcoming, and full of tales at the end of every long day. And of course they offered good food. Teilo loved the melons. Padarn loved the soft, white cheese. And David loved the bread. Thin, round bread, exactly like a plate. Padarn loaded his with a large lump of cheese, an ostrich egg, pistachio nuts, almonds, a pomegranate, and a chicken leg. He ate every scrap, plate and all.

At supper David became friends with a woman called Salome. She showed David a slab of black stone, with a fine carving of a dog and leopard fighting viciously.

'This was a gift from my husband,' said Salome. 'His name was Joash. A stonemason. There was no one to beat him at carving black stone. It's a very hard stone, and almost impossible to carve.'

David eyed the beautiful gift. 'Superb!' he said. In spite of his great enthusiasm David was so tired, all he wanted to do was nod off. His eyes were hot and stinging. He could feel the grit crunch under his eyelids as he rubbed them.

'David, you're half asleep!'

'No, I'm not. I'm wide awake.' What good would he be as a monk if all he could do was make everyone miserable with his moans and groans? 'If I were a caveman I'd be out there beating up the mammoths with the branch of a tree,' said David. 'Tell me your story. I'd love to hear it.'

'It was a Saturday. There had been a strange feeling to the day since early morning. I hadn't been happy ever since I'd heard of the baby who had been born with three ears. It could only mean one thing. The gods were restless.'

'There is only one God, Salome.'

'I know that now, but I'm telling you how things used to be in my life. The mountain was full of gods looking down on us, and each one was restless. That's how it felt.'

'And what happened on this Saturday?' David leaned forward towards Salome, gently but very deliberately. At once she felt she wanted to cry. She swallowed hard two or three times. There was a lump like a melon seed stuck in her throat and it wouldn't budge.

'I had four children. The best in the whole world,' said Salome. 'They had finished their tasks for the day. Hiram at the pottery in the village, working on a jug to store oil. He was so proud of it! Saph worked for the carpenter, Hadad was out hunting, and Cuw had only just finished carving a comb out of a camel's hoof.'

'They must all take after their father,' said David. 'Each one an expert craftsman.'

'They were all excellent craftsmen. But that night, when we had all gone to bed, a terrible thing happened. First we heard a noise. A wild animal.'

'But you're used to hearing the call of wild animals,' said David. 'Bears in the mountains. Leopards. Even wild monkeys.'

'Yes, of course. But this wasn't a far away noise. It was very close. Just outside the wall of the house. Something was out there, growling. Then heavy paws pounded the ground.'

'GRR–RR–R!!'

The door hurtled open. A hungry leopard charged in. He leapt on the four sons and tore them to pieces. Salome screamed. The dog barked. The leopard attacked the terrified dog and mauled it to shreds.

'GRR–RR–R!!'

The leopard calmly wandered out into the night.

In her agitation Salome tipped wine into her lap. She leapt up. Salome dried her dress with her hanky and tried to gather herself. She was all fingers and thumbs.

'There, there,' said David.

'And it was only a cub! A baby!' wailed Salome, tears flowing.

'I know, I know. It's enough to break your heart. Losing the four best sons in the world. And is that why you're going to Jerusalem?'

'To thank God for my sons. And to see where his son, Jesus, was killed. I'll feel much better then. I feel much better now.'

Salome held David's hand and kissed his cheek. 'Thank you, David. Thank you.' David smiled for the first time that day. His cheeks were on fire. In his shyness he had forgotten all about the dust and the heat and the tiredness.

But tomorrow would come soon enough. The last leg of the long journey to Jerusalem. One night's sleep, half a day's journey, and he would be in the Holy City.

David slept like a log all night. When he got up in the morning Salome had left for Jerusalem. It was nearer mid-day when he and Teilo and Padarn reached the Holy City.

Jerusalem was a maze of streets. High buildings threw their cool shadows onto the streets below. David was very excited as his habit brushed against the wicker baskets on one of the bazaar stalls.

'A palm-leaf, sir? A palm-leaf?' called one of the traders. David accepted the badge, his heart pounding. 'Bless you,' said David. 'Which way to the Church

of the Holy Sepulchre?'

'Straight ahead. You can't miss it.'

The three friends enjoyed the noisy bazaar, the myriad stalls, and the thick scent of spices which filled the air. But they had no time for dawdling. Jesus' tomb was situated in an old, fragrant garden a little outside Jerusalem. The three friends walked right into the tomb in the rock. There was a ledge where Jesus' body had been laid to rest, and a large rock which sealed the entrance to the tomb. They looked at each other and smiled. At that very instant the bells rang out through the city of Jerusalem. It was three o'clock in the afternoon. The perfect time to think of Jesus' death.

'Christ died,' said Teilo.

'Christ arose,' said Padarn.

'Christ will return,' said David.

'Blessed be the name of the Lord!'

The noisy synod

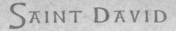

The noisy synod

Its buzz rose like white cotton wool into the cold morning breeze. Chatter, chatter, chatter. No man had ever heard so much chatter.

There were kings there in their linen gowns and their bearskin cloaks, boasting the feats of their soldiers. They boasted how one had pulled a spear from his thigh and had thrown it back at his enemy, having suffered nothing worse than a twinge in his muscle. They boasted how another had attacked a wild Irishman and pinned his skin and bones to the kitchen wall. Non-stop boasting.

Next to the kings stood the young princes in their snakeskin shoes, gossiping about the girls who fancied them.

'Gwenfair has her eye on you? Don't be daft. It's as plain as a pikestaff that she only has eyes for Prince Maelgwn. If she were any the wiser for it. He wouldn't notice if his pants were on fire.'

There was the odd head of curly red hair among the earls and barons who stood next in line, each one with a red tongue to boot – dangling down to his stomach if the noise was anything to go by. They were discussing market prices, and very difficult sums, such as 'How many cows does a gold cup cost?' and 'How long is a tailor's yard?'

'Ask Brychan! Brychan's yard is always the same length. Brychan is an honest man.'

'An honest man, my foot! He's a swindler! I'd rather trust a snake than trust him. He wakes up every morning longing to find a blind man to cheat.'

The clerics stood a little way off, in their rough habits and pigskin sandals. The clerics were godly people but they could chatter away as well as anyone. They loved to predict the future. They hoped these people (too many for anyone to count) would be able to map out the religious life of Wales, once and for all.

There was much to organise. Following the plague, the Yellow Plague, hundreds if not thousands of Welshmen had died, mostly farmers. Hundreds of good monks and church leaders had died too. Without strong leaders the life of an ordinary monk could be pretty lax. Quarrelling and falling out with each other, playing cards by the fire, that was all they thought about lately. The odd one had given in to the very bad habit of spitting into the fire. That was why these good people had come together, in the midst of the beautiful Welsh hills, on that very cold morning.

The sound of a bell, with an enormous tongue, rang throughout the land. A thrill of excitement sprang through the crowd. The Synod of Llanddewibrefi in the year 569 was about to begin.

First on the agenda was choosing the chief monk of the Island of Britain. Quite a task! Whichever monk preached so that everyone in the crowd could hear him would be appointed leader of the church of the Island of Britain. One monk after another preached in his best voice. One roared like a lion. The next mewed like

a kitten. The third whispered like a thin grey mouse, and the fourth bubbled through his sermon with the voice of a lark. One after the other, all morning. Which one would win the title?

No one wanted to be the first to say it. But at last one of the ordinary people called out. 'You're all wasting your time. You're working yourselves up into a sweat for nothing. Not one in every hundred people in this crowd can hear a word of your sermons.'

'Not even one in every thousand!' confirmed another. It was all such a mess. They quarrelled and argued, and there wasn't a bit of order among them for hours on end.

As time went on, it became obvious that no one could preach to such a large crowd without God's help. God would have to strengthen the voice of anyone who hoped to preach to thousands upon thousands of people. Everyone thought hard. Did they know of anyone who could project his voice to the back of the crowd? No. Even a trumpet wouldn't carry to the furthest points, never mind an ordinary voice.

Then Paulinus spoke. He was an old, old monk who looked like a huge cuddly bear in his brown habit and long beard. 'I know of a wonderful young man who loves God, and God loves him. His name is David. Ask him to preach. You won't be disappointed. I'm sure God has given him this rare gift of preaching to enormous crowds of people. If David agrees to preach, I'm certain every man, woman and child will hear him as clearly as if he were standing right next to them.'

Two monks braved the journey from Llanddewibrefi to St David's to look for him. They found him teaching and praying. When David was invited to preach at the synod he was surprised. 'I'd rather stay here to pray. Go back to Llanddewi in the peace and love of God.'

But the synod sent them back to David to persuade him more earnestly to preach to them. It was a wasted journey. David still wouldn't agree.

At the third attempt the synod decided to send two of the holiest monks in Wales to speak to David. Deiniol and Dyfrig set off in fine form. They were certain they could persuade David to come back to Llanddewi with them. The two happy men rested at dusk, prayed together in the light of the moon, and slept soundly all night.

That evening, the exact evening before Deiniol and Dyfrig reached St David's, David sent his monks fishing. 'Catch enough fish to prepare a fine feast for our visitors tomorrow. Bring a bowl of fresh water from the well. They'll be parched after their long journey.'

The monks went down to the beach.

'David must have had some sort of message warning him of these visitors tomorrow,' said the oldest monk. He shook his head in disbelief. 'How odd. I didn't see anyone all day.'

The next day Deiniol and Dyfrig arrived just as the cook was taking the fish out of the large wall-oven. The cook prodded the fish with his fork. The smell of fish poached in garlic butter and fresh herbs cocooned them all. There was a jug of ice cold water on the table. The instant the monks sat down to their meal the water turned into wine.

'Do you eat like this every day?' asked a surprised Deiniol.

'A little bird told me you'd be here by mid-afternoon,' laughed David. 'And he told me what your message would be! But come. Help yourselves to food first. Business can wait until later.'

Dyfrig dug his heels in. 'We won't accept a crumb of food or a drop of wine until you promise us you'll preach at the synod. There's a huge crowd waiting there for you – more than the number of stars in the sky. Please come with us, for the love of God.'

'For the love of God, I'll come. But I won't preach,' warned David. The three monks smiled broadly. Each ate his fill and, for the time being, was content.

How David became the patron saint of Wales

How David became the patron saint of Wales

'Don't you two have anything better to do than gossip like two old hens?' teased David, his handsome face damp and clean and a whiff of lavender playing behind his ears. 'It's you who want me to go to this synod,' he said. 'Let's be going.'

'Don't be such a grumbling old wrinkly,' said Deiniol, punching David in the arm.

What a happy day this would be for David. All day long in the company of his best friends. And a day on the road as well! But as they got nearer the Synod of Llanddewibrefi the three friends could hear someone crying. Nearer and nearer they came, and the crying got louder and louder. They could see a small red dot in the distance. It got bigger and bigger as the three walked towards it. Someone, looking like a scarecrow, was coming to meet them, weeping and wailing for all the world to hear.

'I wonder what the matter is,' said David anxiously.

'You deal with this,' said Deiniol. 'We'll go on to Llanddewibrefi to let them know you're on your way. They must be on tenterhooks by now.'

David waited for the scarecrow. He soon saw that it was a young woman wearing a red dress. She was very frightened.

'Don't be afraid. I'm David. Tell me what's wrong.'

When the red woman heard David's name she fell on her knees before him. 'I've heard that you're a good man, godly and kind. I've heard that you care for the poor, and for people who are in trouble.' The woman cried her eyes out once more. She cried so much, David couldn't understand a word she was saying. He held her hand and stroked it gently. The young woman soon felt better. She wiped her tears and blew her nose.

'A terrible thing has happened. I never thought such a dreadful thing would happen to me.' She started to sniff once more. 'My name is Buddug and I'm a widow. My husband died many years ago. And now my only son has died. O David! What shall I do?'

The sun was high in the sky by the time the woman had finished her story. That very morning her son, Magna, had gone out to work in the fields. He let the cows out to graze. The bull broke loose and attacked Magna furiously in the stomach. There was nothing anyone could do to help. Neighbours carried Magna home and set his body on a bed of straw.

'When I saw the men coming towards the house there was a lump of fear in my heart, growing every minute as they came nearer and nearer. I was sure it was Magna they were carrying in their arms. He was dead. I ran outside to look for a priest to help me. At last I found you.'

'There, there,' said David. 'Let's go back to the house.'

Magna lay there, pale and still. David and Buddug knelt down one on either side of Magna's bed. David prayed. He prayed with such force, he could have uprooted an oak-tree. 'My Lord God, have mercy on this poor widow. Let her son come back to life, and may your name be glorified over the whole earth, for ever and ever.' David prayed so intensely, his warm tears fell on the dead boy's face.

In that instant David could feel some warmth returning to Magna's hand. Magna's fingers twitched. His body quivered like a leaf. Then he opened his eyes. David lifted him up from his bed and gave him to his mother. Magna was in perfect health.

'Thank you, David! Thank you. I believed that my son was dead,' said Buddug. 'From this moment on let him live to serve God and to serve you.'

And that is how David and Magna arrived at the Synod of Llanddewibrefi, late but laughing. Deiniol and Dyfrig had been there for hours and the whole company was looking forward to seeing David.

They had seen him coming from afar and had gone out to meet him. One wanted to see him, another wanted to touch him. One wanted to be blessed by him, another wanted to hug him. One wanted to speak to him, another wanted to worship him. But each one, from the oldest to the youngest, wanted David to preach at the Synod of Llanddewibrefi that day.

'I only promised to come here! I wouldn't dare preach here!' David protested. But David couldn't refuse for very long. They coaxed and cajoled until he finally agreed to teach them more about the life of their precious Lord Jesus.

'Come and stand on this hill, David.' They tried their best to persuade him to stand on the highest piece of ground possible so that they could all see him.

'No, indeed,' said David. 'This flat piece of ground is good enough for me.'

'Then let's make a heap of clothes for you to stand on. It will make it easier for us to see you and to hear you.' They all hurried forward and threw a cloak or a hanky to form a stage for David to stand on.

'It's all right. There's no need for that,' said David patiently. 'But I'll put my own hanky under my feet.' David stood on his clean white hanky. Then, in the sight of all, a snow white dove from heaven settled on David's shoulder. It stayed there the whole time David was preaching. He preached in a loud, clear voice about Jesus the Son of God being born a tiny baby to Mary. He preached about Jesus living a perfect life. He preached about Jesus dying on behalf of his people. And he preached about Jesus coming back to life after death, to be with God in heaven and with men, women and children on earth.

As he preached, an amazing thing happened. The ground under David's feet rose up. Very, very slowly. Higher and higher. Soon the flat earth was a high hill. Everyone could see David as plain as day, and they could all hear his

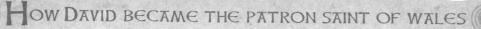

message. He raised his voice and it rang like a trumpet.

They were all amazed. In the heat of the moment each king and cleric knelt to praise God. 'As God has given the salmon to be king of the fish, and the wren to be king of the birds, so God has given David to be leader of the Christians of the Island of Britain,' they said.

And that is how David became the patron saint of Wales.

Do the little things of life!

Do the little things of life!

The spring of that year, the year AD 589, had been very pleasant. The lambing season had been easy, and the flock had grown so large it seemed the hills were alive with sheep. The grain stores had kept all through the winter and there was enough left for everyone to eat bread until high summer. Clear honey flashed in earthenware pots, and there was enough mead in the vats to sink a ship. Yes, all was well.

The monks had only one concern. And it was a great misery for them. David's strength was failing. He was very old. He was very tired. He never wandered the fields any more to watch the monks ploughing. He never milked the cows or fed the calves. All David did was attend church and listen to the services. That was where he enjoyed himself most.

One morning, at matins, an angel spoke to him. 'David,' said the angel, 'do you remember asking God to take you to heaven when you die? Well, that time is near at hand. On the first day of March, be ready!'

David's face lit up with happiness and excitement. But the other monks were confused, and couldn't understand. Was David doting in his old age? Was he chattering away to himself?

'Don't be silly!' said David. 'I was speaking to an angel. An angel came to tell me when I'll die.'

The monks nodded their heads. Not that this was something they were accustomed to. Oh, no. Angels didn't visit the monastery every day of the week, not even to tell David when he would die. And yet, this was a proper thing to do, somehow. An angel speaking to David telling him when he would die. Yes, that was very proper.

It was only Cynan who felt embarrassed. David was so odd. He spoke quietly and gently about dying and going to heaven as if he were telling them he was going to church or down to the beach. Cynan couldn't bear to listen. David knew that. 'Would you rather I didn't tell you these things?' David asked.

Cynan wasn't sure how to answer. He was very upset. Truth to tell, Cynan was afraid of hearing these things, and at the same time he was afraid of not knowing. And on top of everything else he didn't want anyone to know about his dilemma. It was all so very difficult!

'It makes me sad to think of you being so old and weak,' said Cynan. 'I can't imagine living without you in a week's time.'

'God will be with you till the end of time,' said David. 'And remember this: half the things you're afraid of never happen, and the other half are never as bad as you expect them to be.'

The word spread that David was dying. People from far and near visited him. Friends sailed over from Ireland to see him. Some sailed from Brittany and Cornwall. The sea reeled with ships moving quickly towards Porth-clais. Visitors flocked to David like bees making for their hives before a storm. The poor would miss his gifts. The sick would miss his help. Young and old would miss his company. Even the newborn babies would miss him. It was the same everywhere. The old men mourned as if their own son was dying. The young men mourned as if their own father was dying.

On the last Sunday of February David went to church and celebrated his last communion. Then he preached his last sermon. It was his best yet. No one had ever heard such a sermon before, and no one will ever hear such a sermon again. When he had finished celebrating communion and preaching his sermon, David turned to the people and blessed them.

'Brothers and sisters,' he said, 'be full of joy! Keep your faith and guard your belief! Do those little things, which you have learned from me and seen in me.' David smiled. His face was crinkled with happiness.

David didn't see his friends after that. A great weakness came over him and he was carried to bed in the monastery.

On the first day of March, a Tuesday, very early in the morning, a cock crowed. The monks were all in church, at matins, singing hymns and praying. David listened to them from his cell.

David opened his eyes. He was very, very tired. Cynan brought him a drop of water. It was his turn to look after David. David couldn't speak but his eyes were smiling. It was a 'thank-you' smile. Then, without a word, David died.

Cynan looked at him for a long while; at his calm, peaceful face. David was right. Some things turn out much better than expected. David had gone, with joy and in triumph, to the place where there is light without end, and youth without old age, and where the King of kings lives forever more.

Cynan kissed him gently on his forehead.